MOG AT THE ZOO

for Emms

MOG at the ZOO

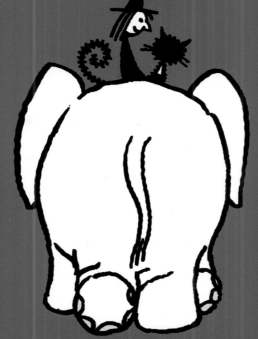

by Helen Nicoll
and Jan Pieńkowski

PUFFIN BOOKS

Meg, Mog and Owl went to the zoo

The keepers looked at Mog

He flew past the flamingos

He zipped past the zebras

and
ran
slap
into
a tree

BOING!

They put Mog in a cage and went

away to look him up in a book

An elephant gave her a bun

The
animals
went
to sleep

Pandemonium broke out

CHATTER

SQUAWK

ROAR

HOWL

MONK

..Squeak

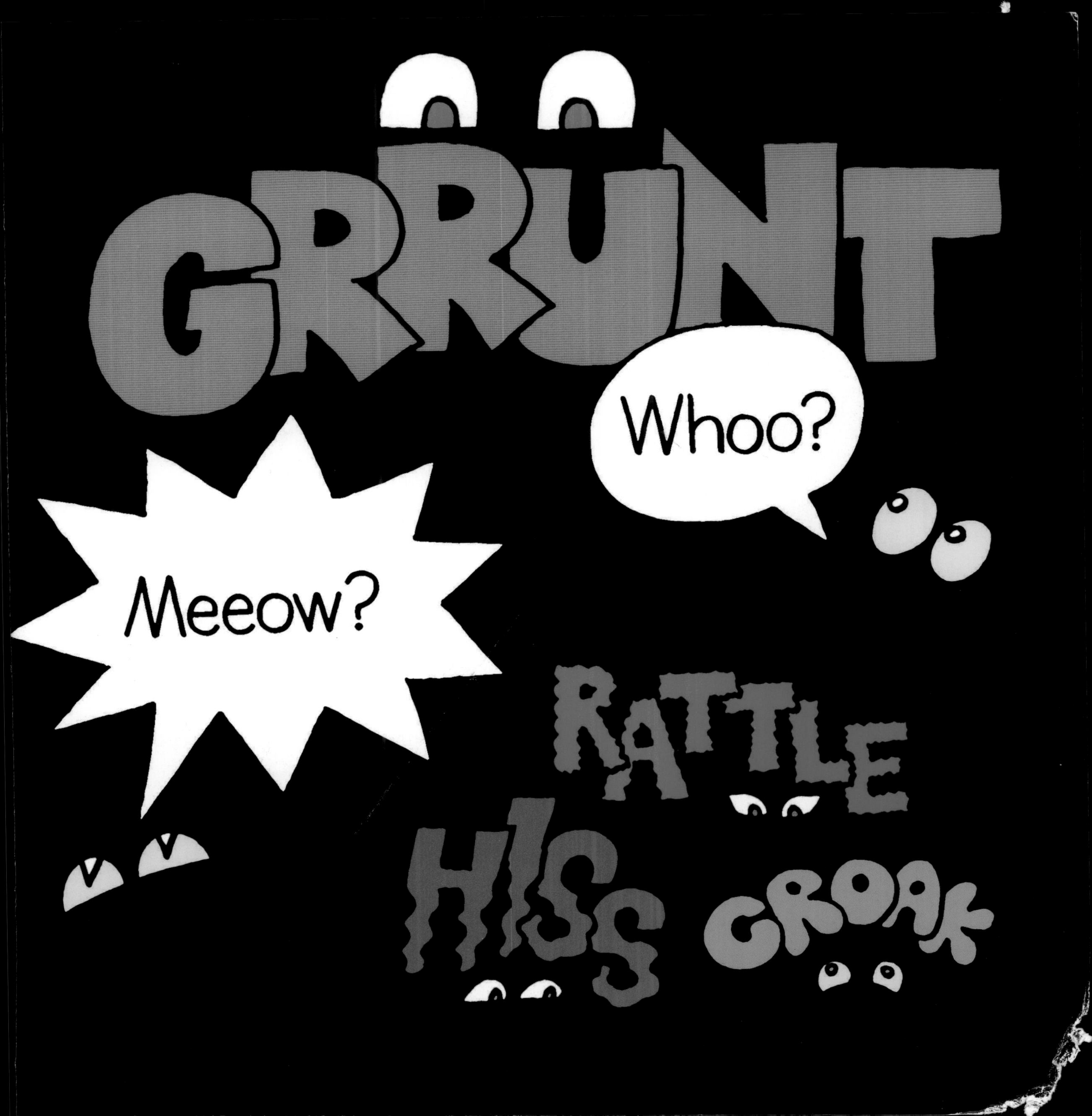
GRRUNT
Whoo?
Meeow?
RATTLE
HISS
CROAK

They had
breakfast
in a
tree

Goodbye!